Violet Mackerel's Pocket Protest

ANNA BRANFORD

illustrated by
SAM WILSON

WALKER BOOKS

First published 2013 by Walker Books Australia Pty Ltd

First published in the UK 2015 by Walker Books Ltd
87 Vauxhall Walk, London SE11 5HJ

2 4 6 8 10 9 7 5 3 1

Text © 2013 Anna Branford
Illustrations © 2015 Sam Wilson

This book has been typeset in Bembo

Printed and bound in Great Britain by Clays Ltd, St Ives plc

British Library Cataloguing in Publication Data:
a catalogue record for this book is available from the British Library

ISBN 978-1-4063-4985-6

www.walker.co.uk

www.violetmackerel.com

For Lisa (my friend)
AB

For Poppy and Lily
SW

The Oak Tree

Violet Mackerel is under the big
old oak tree at Clover Park. She is
collecting acorns with her very good
friend, Rose. So far they have about

twenty each but
they are still looking for
more, mainly because it is nice to be
under the tree when the sun is filtering
through the yellowish-green leaves.

Just as their pockets are getting too full to hold many more acorns, a truck pulls up and two people get out. They are dressed in matching overalls with writing that says **JOHNSON'S TREE SERVICES**.

Rose guesses that tree servicers are a bit like waiters at a restaurant, except instead of bringing drinks on trays they bring them in buckets and hoses. Violet suspects they could be a bit like doctors, only instead of counting heartbeats and listening to chests, they count acorns and listen to rustling leaves. They both think that when they are older they might like to have matching overalls that say **Violet and Rose's Tree Services**.

The people in the van walk over, but they don't have time to explain what they do. They just need Violet and Rose to move out of their way so they can measure different parts of the tree.

Vincent is sitting near by on a wooden bench, reading a book called *Honeymooning on a Shoestring*. He and Violet's mum got married a while ago now but there wasn't enough money for a honeymoon, so they are thinking of having a late one. Violet has had lots of good ideas for them, like scuba diving in the ocean or going to space. But there is still not much money, so they definitely need the shoestring sort of honeymoon. That is why Vincent and Violet borrowed the book from the library.

Violet and Rose both feel slightly shy after being asked to move away from the oak tree, so they join Vincent on the bench and look at the book. The bench is their second favourite place in the park because it has a nice goldish plaque that says IN MEMORY OF EVA.

It twinkles as if the dusty old wood is wearing a brooch and they like wondering who Eva might have been.

"What do you think those people are doing?" Violet asks Vincent.

But before he can answer, the woman calls out, asking if there is a petrol station near by. Vincent is a bit deaf so he has to go up quite close to hear her properly and they end up talking.

"Did they tell you anything?" asks Rose, when he joins them back on the bench.

"Yes," says Vincent, frowning. "They told me they've been hired to cut the oak tree down."

"Cut it down?" checks Violet.

"Cut it right down?" double-checks
Rose.

Vincent nods. "There is going to be
a car park built over this part of the
park and they need to clear the land
before laying down the concrete."

"They can't do that!" says Violet.

"Unfortunately they can," says Vincent. "They're coming back in two weeks to do the job."

It is an extremely nasty surprise.

Before leaving, the people from **JOHNSON'S TREE SERVICES** bang a big sign onto the tree with a staple gun. It says **PUBLIC NOTICE – TREE REMOVAL**.

It is quite late in the day now and
the birds are getting noisy. The cicadas
have started singing and the insects
are turning golden in the setting
sunlight. Vincent, Violet and Rose
do the slow, quiet walking that
people do after they
find out something
worrying.

When they
get home,
Violet and
Rose go up
to Violet's
room to think.

They have told each other their best secrets under the oak tree. They have found some good small things there too – not just acorns, but a leaf skeleton and a butterfly wing and even a golden coin. It is hard to imagine the park without the oak tree.

"Do you have any theories that might help?" asks Rose.

Violet has theories about lots of things and they are sometimes useful for solving problems. Violet thinks.

"No," she says. "Maybe it's because my theories are mostly about small things and this is an extremely big thing."

Rose thinks too.

"Vincent said the chopping won't actually happen for two weeks," she says.

"There must be something we can do before then."

Violet agrees, but she doesn't know what the something could be. That is the problem.

The
Enormous Protest

At dinnertime it is just
Violet, Vincent and
Violet's big sister, Nicola,
because Rose has
gone home and
Mum and Violet's
brother, Dylan, are
at a violin recital.

They talk about the problem of the oak tree. Vincent says he is going to write a letter to the local newspaper, which Violet thinks is a very good idea. But she is still hoping for an idea of her own.

"You could try holding a protest," Nicola says. "Lara and I organized one at school last year."

Violet remembers Nicola and Lara's protest. The sports department had planned to turn one of the art studios into

a sports equipment room because
there wasn't enough space for all their
hoops and wickets and they said hardly
anyone was using it. But Nicola and
her best friend Lara did use it, almost
every day. So they collected a petition
which, they told Violet, is a long list
of names and signatures of people
who think something is important.
They dressed up as artists in berets
and smocks and carried big cardboard
signs that said **SAVE OUR STUDIO**
and **RIGHTS FOR ARTISTS NOW**.
They marched around the school doing
a chant they made up, which Violet
remembers because they practised it
a lot in Nicola's room.

One, two, three, four,
Where are we supposed to draw –
Four, three, two, one,
When our studio is gone?
Five, six, seven, eight,
We need spaces to create –
Eight, seven, six, five,
Keep art in our school alive!

It was a very good
chant, Violet thought.

After dinner, Violet, Vincent and Nicola watch a television show about holidays. Vincent is hoping there might be a shoestring section, but the show is more the sort with hotels and spas and towels cleverly folded into the shapes of birds. Violet wishes there could be bird towels on Mum and Vincent's honeymoon.

Nicola has lent Violet a scrapbook with pictures of her and Lara protesting, their petition and some of the letters they wrote. Violet watches the television with one eye and looks at the scrapbook with the other. But her mind's eye is seeing herself and Rose leading an enormous protest wearing costumes. Violet has a tree costume with branches and leaves, and Rose has a bird costume with eggs and a built-in nest. They are marching around the park, holding a big sign that says SAVE OUR OAK TREE.

Their petition is as thick as an encyclopedia. A huge crowd of people follow them and some are dressed up too, as trees, birds and other animals whose natural habitat is the oak tree (although their costumes are not as nice as Violet and Rose's). They are doing a special tree-saving chant which Violet's mind's ear can't quite hear yet.

But her mind's eye is doing a brilliant job of seeing a little plane writing

Say no to chopping

across the sky above the park. It would be an excellent protest, Violet thinks.

It is nearly bedtime, so Violet says thank you to Nicola for the idea and goes up to her room. She wishes it was not too late to tell Rose about the enormous protest and the little plane.

When Mum gets back from the violin recital she comes upstairs to say goodnight and Violet tells her about the oak tree and the car park and **JOHNSON'S TREE SERVICES**.

"Do you think there is any chance we will be able to save the oak tree?" Violet asks.

"If the decision has already been made, then probably only a very small chance," says Mum. "But it's always worth trying, if something is important."

Mum has some holiday brochures in her hand and Violet suspects she is thinking of the honeymoon as well as the oak tree. But as she goes to sleep, she thinks about what Mum has said. The oak tree is important. It is worth trying.

The Small Sign

The next morning is Saturday, which
is market day for the Mackerels and
Vincent. They have a stall
with Mum's knitted things
on one side and Vincent's
CHINA BIRDS on the
other and Violet
usually helps

with both. But this
morning she is
going to Rose's
house instead. She
is going to take her

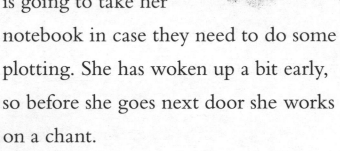

notebook in case they need to do some
plotting. She has woken up a bit early,
so before she goes next door she works
on a chant.

She would like to write one with
numbers like Nicola and Lara's, so she
starts by writing One, two, three, four
in her notebook. There are not many
oak-tree related words that rhyme
with four. But Violet has been doing
fractions at school, so she has the idea
of trying those. She writes One, two,

two-and-a-half, three, which turns out
to rhyme with Please do not
chop down our tree.

Violet smiles.

Rose and her mum are
having breakfast smoothies
when Violet arrives and
there is enough for Violet to
have one too. Violet
explains to Rose
about the petition
and she also tells
her about the plane.
Rose especially likes the
chant. Rose's mum says there
is some cardboard in the recycling so
they start by making a sign.

They find two cereal boxes which
they open out and stick together with
sticky tape to make one biggish piece
of cardboard. On the grey side where
there aren't any pictures of cereal,
Rose writes SAVE OUR OAK TREE
because her writing is the neatest and
Violet draws the tree because her tree
drawings are quite good. They have
to leave a space where the sticky tape

is because the pens don't draw there.
Violet and Rose look carefully at their
work. It is not a bad sign. But it is not
much like the one in their minds' eyes.

Rose frowns.

"I think for an enormous protest,
what we need is a really big sign," she
says, "so everyone will see it and want
to join us. I'm not sure if anyone will
notice a small, greyish sign."

Violet thinks.

"Rose," she says, "you and I would notice a small sign, no matter what colour it was."

"We would especially notice a sign if it was small," agrees Rose.

"And we are the sort of people who mind a lot about things like tree chopping."

Rose nods and Violet thinks a bit more.

Then Violet has an idea. She writes in her notebook. It is called the **Theory of Seeing Small Signs** and it goes like this. The kind of people who might notice small signs are exactly the sort who probably care most about small things (such as birds not having nests and people not having a place to collect acorns).

Rose smiles. "That is a very good theory," she says.

Although the cereal boxes were the biggest pieces of cardboard in Rose's recycling, there are lots of smaller pieces that are not grey and do not have pictures on them. They are perfect for making small signs that say things like

RIGHTS FOR BIRDS

TREES PLEASE

and

NESTS ARE BEST

which are quite catchy, and there is still space underneath to write SAVE OUR OAK TREE, so people will know exactly what they mean. Violet and Rose make a lot of small signs while they practise the fractions chant.

TREES PLEASE
SAVE OUR
OAK TREE

The
Wet Floor

Late that afternoon when Mum and
Vincent are back from the market and
have unpacked and had a cup of tea,
Vincent takes Violet and
Rose to Clover Park
again. Their small signs
are just the right size to
carry in their pockets.

They put a few of them in special places along the path that runs through the park and Vincent helps with the high-up places. Violet and Rose do their chant, even though no one is there to hear it except Vincent. They also do a sort of protesting dance, which ends up going around the trunk of the oak tree.

"Don't worry, ants," calls Violet to three small black ones crawling up the trunk. "We're going to save your home."

"Don't worry, birds," calls Rose up into the branches. "We're going to save your nests."

If Violet and Rose stop dancing
and stand on opposite sides of the tree
and give it a big hug, they find that
they can hold hands around it.

"Don't worry, oak tree," whispers
Violet into the scratchy bark.

"We are doing our best to help,"
whispers Rose.

They stay under the oak tree
for a long time.

Violet saves the
last of the small signs
to tweak between the
wooden slats under the EVA
brooch on the bench.

After that,
they look
around at
the protest
they have
begun. It
is different from the
enormous one their minds'

eyes first saw. This is more of a pocket
protest. But they are both feeling very
hopeful about the **Theory of Seeing**
Small Signs.

Perhaps someone who cares about small things will spot one of the signs and know exactly what to do to save the oak tree. Even though the wind is picking up and the leaves are starting to rustle together, hardly any of the signs are blowing away.

Vincent is feeling hopeful too. He and Mum sold lots of china birds and knitted things at the market this morning. They really might be able to do one or two of the ideas in his honeymoon book.

But after they say goodbye to Rose, there is some bad news waiting for Violet and Vincent, which is rather a lot of water on the floor. Mum and

Nicola are mopping
it with towels, and
Dylan is building
a dam of socks
in the laundry
doorway to
stop it flowing out. Everyone is in a
slight panic.

"The washing machine leaked," says
Mum, handing some dripping towels
to Vincent to wring out over the sink.

Violet adds more socks to Dylan's
sock dam and watches the water
puddling in the laundry.

It seems like a proper flood at first,
but the water has not leaked past the
sock dam so it doesn't take long to

clean up. But Mum and Vincent look
gloomy.

Vincent says it will be hard to get
by in a house with five people and
no washing machine. If they all wear
socks every day, by the end of one
week that is seventy socks (which
is why Dylan and Violet were able
to build such a good dam). The
Mackerels and Vincent wear a lot of
other clothes besides socks too. Mum
says the washing machine is beyond

repair and they will have to use the
honeymoon savings to buy a new one.

"Oh, well," she sighs. "It was fun
thinking about the honeymoon
anyway." Vincent gives her a hug.

Mum puts the holiday brochures and
her list of honeymoon ideas
away in a drawer.

Violet is sad that Mum
and Vincent will not be
having a honeymoon,
not even the shoestring sort.

There is also another reason Violet is feeling glum. The small wind that was rustling the leaves at the park is turning into a big one, and rain is starting to patter against the window. Normally that is a sound Violet especially likes. But not when she is thinking of small signs blowing and washing away.

Violet makes one last small sign on a piece of paper from her notebook, just to cheer herself up. She writes RIGHTS FOR HONEYMOONERS. In the corner she draws a towel, folded into the shape of a bird. Before she goes to bed, she sticks the sign onto the fridge.

The **Theory of** Small **Signs** might be trickier than it first seemed. Not even Violet or Rose would notice a small sign in the park that had been washed or blown away. And the only people who will see the honeymoon sign on the fridge are her family. They

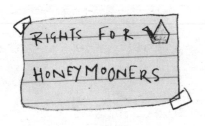

all wanted Mum and Vincent to have a honeymoon anyway.

The
Acorn Messages

The next morning, it is
still drizzling, but there
is a cheering smell
coming from the
kitchen because
Sunday is the
day that Vincent
makes pancakes.

Today he is making extra because his friend Buzz is coming over, and Buzz never says no to a pancake. Neither does Rose, who arrives under a beautiful umbrella that her dad brought back from Japan. It is a bit like an upside-down teacup with no handle.

After breakfast, Violet and Rose help with washing up while Vincent and Buzz carry the broken washing machine out to Buzz's truck.

"I think our small signs probably floated away in the rain last night," Rose says to Violet, as soon as they are alone in Violet's room.

"Maybe the **Theory of Small Signs** is not such a good theory after all," says Violet.

Rose thinks. "Or maybe it is a very good theory," she suggests, "but we need to try it another way."

It is nice, when you are not feeling

hopeful, if someone else is feeling
hopeful enough for two.

"The problem," says Rose, "is that
small signs are not waterproof. I wish
we had lots of mini umbrellas."

Violet looks at Rose's beautiful
Japanese umbrella. "I think I might be
having an idea," she says.

Violet still has the pocketful of
acorns from the oak tree. She had been
going to turn the cups into hats for
the dolls in her shoebox doll's house.
Violet likes the way acorn cups look
like hats. But now she is thinking
that they might work slightly
like umbrellas too.

She gets out her notebook and using tiny writing, writes Save the Clover Park oak tree! in one straight line.

She cuts the line out carefully with her scissors. Then she rolls it round her little finger. She takes an acorn out of its cup and puts the small message inside. It uncurls to fit perfectly around the inside of the cup.

Rose smiles and turns it upside

down. It is the perfect hiding spot for a small message and it is also a perfect umbrella.

Rose writes The Clover Park oak tree needs your help! in her notebook. Then she cuts it out, curls it and puts it in another of the cups.

It takes a long time, but Violet and Rose do not stop until all of the acorn cups have small messages curled inside them. Then Rose runs home and brings back the pocketful that she collected from the oak tree and they put messages in those too. It is a big job, but they don't mind at all.

In the afternoon, Rose has her swimming lesson, so she is going to leave an acorn message in the changing room at the pool and another at the machine where you can buy crisps.

After Rose has gone home to change into her swimming costume, Violet goes with Mum to take a basket of knitted autumn leaves to her friend's shop that sells knitted things. Violet tucks a message acorn cup in among the woolly leaves. Then she puts another on the head of a small knitted doll. Most people would probably mistake it for an

ordinary doll's hat. But
another sort of person
might notice it there and
pick it up and look inside.

Later on, when Vincent goes to
the post box to post the letter about
the oak tree to the local newspaper,
Violet goes with him so she can leave
an acorn message on the step of a little
chapel they pass and another beside the
post box.

The
Short Petition

The next few days are school days
so there is not much time to go to
the park as there is homework in the
evenings and everyone is busy. Violet
and Rose both keep acorn messages
in their pockets so they can leave one
whenever they
see a perfect spot.

They go to different schools so it is interesting to hear about each other's hiding places. On the afternoons when they don't see each other because Rose is horseriding or at the dentist, or Violet has gone with Mum to her knitting group, they leave notes in a special hole they once discovered in the fence between their two back gardens. They say things like:

Dear Violet,

Today I left an acorn message in the ball box at the tennis court and another in the shampoo aisle at the supermarket. Did you find any good places?

Love from Rose

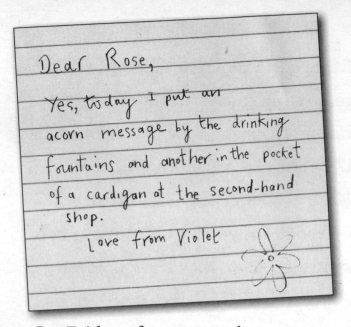

Dear Rose,

Yes, today I put an acorn message by the drinking fountains and another in the pocket of a cardigan at the second-hand shop.

Love from Violet

On Friday afternoon, when no one has anything important they need to do and Vincent doesn't mind going to Clover Park, Violet and Rose are excited to see if anything interesting has happened. Perhaps a few people will have read their acorn messages by now and who knows what sorts of things they might have done to help?

Most of all, they are hoping that the big tree removal sign will have been taken down and perhaps a small sign left in its place that says **PUBLIC NOTICE – TREE TO STAY**.

But, actually, when they arrive at the oak tree everything is exactly as it was before. The notice is still up and it still says **TREE REMOVAL**. There are no protesters gathering or news reporters saying into their microphones, "Plans to remove the oak tree have been abandoned due to a successful pocket protest including small signs and acorn messages. This is Isobel Albatross reporting from Clover Park."

It is all a bit disappointing.

Violet and Rose look around to see if they can spot any of their small signs from last weekend. They only find two, which have blown into the bushes and are much too crumpled and rained-on to be read. Even the one Violet tweaked between the wooden slats of the bench with the brooch is gone. That is the most discouraging thing of all.

Violet and Rose lie quietly under the oak tree and look up into the leafy branches and think together.

Suddenly Rose says, "What about
the petition?"

It sounds a bit like a sneeze, so Violet
says "Bless you", and they both giggle,
which makes them feel a bit better.

"Maybe if there was a long list of people who agree with us, it would help," says Rose.

So Violet takes out her notebook and writes at the top of the page,

We do NOT think it is a good idea to chop down the oak tree.
If you agree, please sign your name.
Violet
Rose

Underneath, Violet writes her name and draws a small violet and Rose signs her name and draws a small rose.

They ask Vincent if he would like
to sign the petition too and he says he
would. But that is only three names,
which is not a very long petition.

Rose thinks. "One evening my mum
and I were driving home past the park
and we saw a bat in the tree. I bet it
would want to help."

Since bats can't write, Rose writes
"Bat" underneath Vincent's signature
in the sort of swooping writing
that bats would probably have if
they could write. Then Violet has
the idea of writing "Bees", which
she has sometimes seen buzzing in
the low branches. She writes it in
buzzing letters. They also add some

sparrows, some ants, two grasshoppers, a butterfly, a moth, a black cat and a friendly huntsman spider. Then, after the small animals' and insects' signatures, they write "probably" in brackets because Vincent says you can't actually add extra names to petitions, although he is sure that the animals would sign if they could.

Even with the added names it is still a short petition, but it is much better than nothing. Rose slides the top of the page under the notice on the tree so that it dangles down underneath, which will hold it there for a short while at least. Perhaps no one will notice it. Perhaps more rain will come

and wash it away. But for the moment,
it is the only other idea Rose and
Violet have for their protest.

The New Names

It is an early morning start for everyone in the Mackerel house the next day. Mum has three big baskets of knitted things

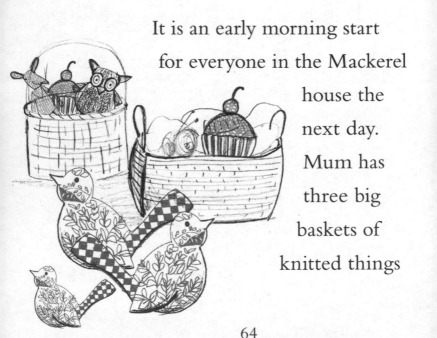

and Vincent has a new batch of CHINA BIRDS that he has been cleaning. Nicola, who sells her handmade jewellery at the market, has a lot of earrings ready too because she is saving up to buy an easel for her room. Dylan will be busking on his

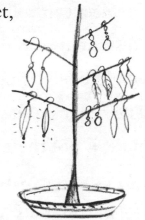

violin. And Violet, who has been too busy with small signs and acorn messages to have anything of her own to bring to the market, will be helping everyone and eating poffertjes.

Vincent and Violet go outside into the garden in their slippers to get the newspaper. They are hoping the newspaper might have published Vincent's letter about the oak tree.

Vincent unrolls the paper and they go straight to the letters section. It would be exciting to see his name. They check a few times to make sure, but it is not there.

"Perhaps it will be published next week," suggests Mum.

"That will be too late," says Vincent.

"The oak tree will be gone by then," says Violet.

Violet helps everyone to load the boxes, baskets, tables and big umbrella into the van, and they drive to the market.

It is a nice morning when the sun comes out, and Violet matches the china birds with all the right knitted nests. But mostly, even while she is eating poffertjes, she is thinking about the oak tree. Vincent is not smiling much. Violet suspects he is thinking about the oak tree too.

When they all get home, there is a surprise on the doorstep, which is Rose wearing a beautiful spotty dress. Violet is not surprised about the dress because she knows Rose has been at a birthday party. But she is surprised to see her waiting on the doorstep. Rose is flapping a piece of paper in her hand.

"Look, look!" squeals Rose as Violet clambers out from the van.

It is the short petition they left on the oak tree. Violet looks, and sees right away why Rose is so excited. There are two new names on the petition, printed in neat, curly, old-fashioned writing.

ALBERT TRIVELLI
and
EVA TRIVELLI (PROBABLY)

"We drove past the park on our way home from the party," says Rose, "so I asked Mum if I could hop out and check the petition, and then I saw it!"

Later in the afternoon, Mum, Nicola and Dylan add their names to the petition, which makes it longer. And after that, Violet, Rose and Vincent go back to the park and put the slightly longer petition back underneath the tree removal sign.

It is hard to know what to think. On the one hand, there is only a week to go until the oak tree will be chopped, the newspaper did not publish Vincent's letter and no one seems to have noticed the pocket protest. These are not especially cheering thoughts. But on the other hand, Albert Trivelli and Eva Trivelli (probably) have seen the short petition.

Perhaps they are the sort of people who will mind about the tree and find a good way to help. That is an extremely cheering thought.

As well as sitting under the oak tree watching the insects go golden for a while, in case it is the last weekend they can, Violet and Rose also sit with Vincent on the bench and look closely at the goldish plaque that that says

IN MEMORY OF EVA

The Sunday Special

Even on Sundays there
is not much sleeping in
for anyone at Violet's house and usually
the waking up of people is done by
Violet, who would like someone
to help her open the marmalade or
explain what a piccolo is. But this
morning it is Vincent who wakes

Violet up by sitting down on her bed with a slight bounce and a newspaper rustling in his hand.

"Look! Look!" Vincent is saying. Violet opens her eyes just a crack.

"Did they publish your letter?" she asks sleepily.

"Better than that!" says Vincent.

Violet rubs her eyes and sits up so she can look. When she sees the paper, she wonders if she is actually still asleep and dreaming. There is a huge picture of the oak tree. And beside the picture is not just Vincent's letter. There are lots of letters. So many that instead of publishing them with the ordinary letters on Saturday, they have all been saved up for a Sunday Special. And in the special, there is a whole section about the mystery acorn messages.

"I had no idea there were plans to cut down the beautiful old tree that my sisters and I played in as children," writes one lady who found an acorn message at the library.

"The oak tree is the nicest part of the view from my office. It would be a terrible shame to lose it," writes a man who found an acorn message at his bus stop.

Vincent and Violet are so busy reading the letters out to each other and gasping and making sure that they both are really, truly awake that it takes them a while to notice what is on the opposite page.

It is another photo, but with tattered edges. At first Violet thinks it must be a different oak tree because it is smaller and has houses with gardens behind it instead of the block of flats that is behind Clover Park. Underneath the tree are a man and a woman with old-fashioned clothes and hats and big smiles. Across the bottom of the photo, someone has written *Albert and Eva Trivelli, 1948*, in faded curly writing.

"Eighty-six-year-old Albert Trivelli was twenty-one when he and his wife, Eva, bought their first home," reads Vincent. "They were married

at Clover Chapel and lived in a house
with a garden looking out onto the
park. Some years later they opened
Chateau Trivelli, a hotel still run by
their son, Henry."

Then Violet reads out one of the parts
where Albert is being interviewed.

"After my wife died, I moved into a
smaller home only a short walk away
and our old house was knocked down
to make room for some flats.

But I still walk to the park most evenings to watch the colours in the oak tree changing as the sun goes down, because that was something Eva and I always did together. I built the bench there in memory of her.

I was terribly sad to see that the tree was to be removed and to think that no one would mind but me. But then I found a small sign on the bench near Eva's name and I realized that at least one other person minded. Then, when I found a petition, I realized that a few did. Even if the oak tree is removed, it is a great comfort to me to know that other people think it is as beautiful and special as I do."

At the end of the article, Vincent reads, "In light of the concerns of local residents, THE CLOVER TIMES has been in contact with the council to discuss the preservation of the oak tree at Clover Park."

Vincent twirls Violet all the way to where Mum is still trying to be asleep. But she wakes up quickly and she doesn't mind them excitedly reading the letters out to her.

The Evening Walk

Violet, Rose and Vincent decide they will go to the park slightly later than normal to see if Albert Trivelli comes to watch the colours changing in the oak tree as the sun goes down. They would all like to meet him. Vincent says if they arrive at about the time they normally

leave, they might find him. Violet and
Rose think it is an excellent idea.

There is no one at the park when
they arrive but they decide to sit and
wait for a while, just in case.

When the green leaves are starting
to turn slightly purple in the changing
light, a man appears on the path. He is
much older than the man in the photo
in the newspaper and he walks
with a stick. But he is wearing

a hat and Violet and Rose
wonder if it is Albert
Trivelli. They smile and
wave, and he smiles and waves
back. After that, they feel sure.
Because he walks slowly and it
is too exciting to wait for him,
they run over to say hello.

"Was it you who made the small
signs and the petition?" Albert asks
Violet and Rose.

"Yes!" they answer together.

Albert shows them the sign they
had tweaked between the slats of the
bench. It has been folded in his pocket.

"It cheers me up every time I look at
it," he tells them.

It is a bit of a squish with all four of them on Eva's bench but they do eventually fit. And Albert shows them how, after turning gold and then purple, the leaves go almost navy blue before they turn into black shadows against the darkening sky.

"Will you come back to our house and have a cup of tea?" asks Vincent, when there are no more colours to see.

"Well, why not?" says Albert.

They walk more slowly than usual so that Albert can keep up. He tells them a story about how he and Eva once hung a rope swing from the oak tree for their son Henry when he was small and how he did such amazing tricks on it that the neighbours thought he was a monkey. Violet and Rose get the giggles.

Violet and Mum made a ginger cake not long ago and there is enough left for everyone to have a slice and when Rose's mum comes to collect her she decides to stay for a piece too.

When they are all busy chatting, Albert says quietly to Violet, "Is that another one of your small signs?"

He is pointing to the RIGHTS FOR HONEYMOONERS sign she put on the fridge on the night of all the rain.

So Violet explains about the shoestring book and the leaky washing machine and the **Theory of Seeing Small Signs**.

"I see," says Albert.

Then Rose's mum asks him about the hotel and he tells them about a special herb garden he and Eva planted there and the French chef who cooks lovely meals for the guests.

Much later on, Vincent says he will drive Albert home. "Before I go," Albert says to Mum and Vincent, "could I offer you both a couple of nights in the honeymoon suite at Chateau Trivelli, to say thank you for everything you have

done to save the oak tree? I don't suppose it will be much of a honeymoon really though, since it's only down the road."

Violet and Rose both squeak with excitement and Mum squeaks slightly too.

"It would be a wonderful honeymoon!" says Mum.

Vincent shakes Albert's hand and says "Thank you" a lot of times, and Mum nearly shakes his hand but then gives him a hug instead.

A hotel with a beautiful garden and a special French chef will be a perfect honeymoon for Mum and Vincent, Violet thinks, still squeaking.

Before Vincent and Albert leave, she whispers a small and secret suggestion into Albert's ear. She has taken the sign down from the fridge and she points to

the picture she drew in
the corner of a towel
folded cleverly into the
shape of a bird.

  "I think that can be
arranged," Albert whispers back.

The New Chant

Next weekend at Rose's
house, when she and Violet
have finished dinner and
are making up a trundle
bed for Violet to sleep
in, the phone rings and
it is Mum. She and Vincent are at
the *Chateau Trivelli* and she wants
to tell Violet all about the delicious

French dinner and the spa and, most especially, the towels that are folded like perfect birds.

In the background, Violet can hear Vincent saying, "Let me talk to her!"

"Vincent has some exciting news too," says Mum, laughing and saying goodbye.

"I just got a message from THE CLOVER TIMES," says Vincent.

Violet holds the phone so Rose can listen to the message too.

"Because of the protest, the council has agreed to build the car park somewhere else," says Vincent.

"They're not cutting down the oak tree?" checks Rose.

"They're definitely not cutting it down?" double-checks Violet.

"Yes!" says Vincent. "You saved it!"

"One, two, two-and-a-half, three – Rose and Violet saved the tree!" chants Violet, bouncing up and down on the trundle bed.

"*Three, four, four-and-a-half, five –*
Nests and acorns all survive!" chants
Rose, scattering pink-and-white
cushions all over her room.

They can hear Vincent and Mum
laughing at the
other end of the
phone and soon
Rose's mum comes
upstairs to see what all
the excitement is.

They have hot
chocolate with
marshmallows to
celebrate.

Later on, when Vincent and Mum
are back from their honeymoon and
Violet, Rose and Vincent start going
to the park in the afternoons again,

they sometimes go a bit later than they used to. Even though it is a squish, they like sitting on the bench with Albert, watching the oak tree's leaves go from gold, to purple, to navy blue and finally to black shadows against the darkening sky.

And if they stay out very late, Violet sometimes notices the small golden sign that Albert made for Eva, twinkling in the moonlight.

IN MEMORY OF EVA

More

stories to collect:

Violet hatches
a plot!

Violet has
her tonsils
out. Ouch!

Violet learns about nature.

Violet's family move house.

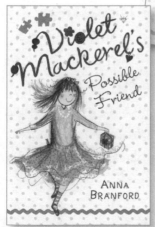

Violet finds a new friend.

ANNA BRANFORD was born on the Isle of Man, but spent her childhood in Sudan, Papua New Guinea and Australia. Once, when she was very itchy with the chicken pox, her dad read her *The Very Hungry Caterpillar* thirty times in a row.

Anna lectures in Sociology at Victoria University, Australia, and spends her evenings writing children's stories, kept company by a furry black cat called Florence. She also makes dolls using recycled fabric and materials.

SAM WILSON graduated from Kingston University and has worked on lots of grown-up books. The Violet Mackerel books are the first titles she has illustrated for children. She says, "I have always wanted to illustrate for children, it has been such fun drawing Violet, she is a gorgeous character with such an adventurous spirit." Sam lives in the countryside with her husband, two children, a black Lab called Jess and several chickens.